Apeman

by

Gerald St Clare

With special thanks to Gordana & David

ISBN: 978-1-64136-598-7

Published by Silversphere Media
A Division of the Sovereign Media Group.

© 2017 All rights reserved

No part of the publication may be reproduced, distributed or transmitted in any form or by any means, including photocopying, recording or other electronic or mechanical methods, without the prior written permission of the publisher, except in the case of brief quotations embodies in the critical reviews and certain other non-commercial uses permitted by copyright law.

All characters and events portrayed in this work are fictional. Any resemblance to any persons living or dead is purely coincidental.

Apeman

My name is Anthony Farrah and, yes you are right, I am that Anthony Farrah, the one who defended the mass-murdering apeman. But before I explain myself, let me tell the story for those who come after us; those who may not know who we were or how we lived.

In the year 2864 of the pre-diaspora calendar (PDC), I was born into the service caste on Arkship AS337.

The Arkships had left Earth from 2192 PDC until about 2283 PDC (the date all communication from Earth ceased). The first few were built and launched in the hope that humans could escape the death of our only planet, either through depletion of resources, man-made destruction of the environment or catastrophic external events. These early ships carried five to ten Leader caste families totalling fifty people, a few hundred staff to look after them, 200 or so live meat animals and frozen seed banks for the destination plants, animals and around 20 million human embryos.

But by the time AS12 was boosting away from Lunar orbit in 2221, our ancestors had realised the cost of just fixing the world was far less than the cost of running away. If only they had worked that out two hundred years earlier, there would have been so much more to save.

So the new Arkship range starting with AS013 were built solely with the intention of spreading humanity (rather than specific humans) to the stars. Notice how the zero was added by the Public Relations team to suggest a long future. The crews of the 013+ Arkships now numbered only eighty: four manager caste, sixty service caste and a dozen or so apemen. The Leader caste no longer had to suffer generations of death in space, they could be born after planet-fall and only once a comfortable environment had been set up by the workers. With a much smaller "live" population and no need for the comforts of the earlier ships, Arkships could be built, stocked, crewed and launched at a rate ten times faster than the old "pre-teen" ships.

The human embryos in storage on these later ships still had the same mix of castes and the biodiversity necessary for a healthy and growing destination population, but a small percentage were also designated as crew members. In the nine hundred years that our journey would take, sufficient managers and service crew were available as embryos to replace their ageing predecessors. Apemen were also replaced, albeit at a much higher rate due to their shorter lifespans.

Our home, the Arkship AS337, was the three hundred and thirty-sixth of her family (we don't count the unfortunate AS017, of course). A shell of safety cocooning a living and near-living cargo which represented the hope of an entire world. That world did not yet have a name.

Apeman

Although the old-earthers probably had a name for the star it orbited, the privilege of naming was reserved for the first Leaders born on that planet. It was an ancient human tradition that the naming of something was a divine permission to ownership of that object. And only a Leader can own a planet.

We called it "new earth"; the lack of capitalisation ensuring that we referred only to the objective, not it's name. My guess is that all Arkship destinations had that same label.

So born into the service caste, I was designated as a geneticist following my 16th year exams. Unlike the old-world geneticists, my role had nothing to do with research or original thought; I simply selected and prepared embryos for birth.

Central Planning would provide weekly reports of the current population status. These included details of personnel health, injuries and any behavioural events over the preceding week. I would take this raw data and calculate recommendations for retirement which were sent back to Central Planning. I also used the retirement and death-in-service data for my own planning; selecting an appropriate genome for each of the personnel that would need to be replaced within the next sixteen years. Management personnel were not retired, so we always needed an excess of them in case of unexpected deaths (only one was actually needed but we ran with four). Service personnel were easier to plan for, with both a larger pool taking up any variation and also the ability to foresee their retirement date in advance.

And apemen were the easiest of all; reaching working age after only five years and any deaths covered by just redistributing their workload; we simply had a few in progress at all times.

Or at least we did until my client went on his rampage...

That Thursday I was working in my lab on a complex splice. The process for every splice was identical and mostly automated, but the importance of every detail being precise and correct made it a high-stress function of my job. (Of course when I say "high-stress", I don't mean I have any recessive tendency, it's just metaphoric).

The door beeped and I started cleaning up. I never answered the door immediately as it was always a Learning Group and the mentor would know that I had to complete any important process and make safe before risking contamination from external agents. But the door just opened! Without my pass-phrase, it just opened and someone came in!

As you can see, I was horrified. I turned on the intruder with fury (metaphoric again, of course). And stopped short.

The woman who had entered was not wearing the normal blue one-piece that every other human I had ever met wore. She was dressed in an exotic garb: a brilliant white shirt, almost blinding to the eye and a long tube of grey fabric reaching from the waist to just below where she probably had knees. I cast the thought of knees from my mind, embarrassed at such an inappropriate thought about someone who was clearly Management. Her features were the classic C1197 line, a genome I had always dreamed of working with. Clearly this was the Rozinia Ferrante I knew from the data: C1197, 28 years old, 88% efficiency, negative events four. She looked angry.

"Did you hear me Anthony?"

I hadn't. "Yes".

Her attention bored through my lie and read my thoughts. "I said 'you have been selected'"

My eyes immediately welled up with tears. I fought it down and tried to understand. I was party to all Planning decisions about retirement and knew I was not even nearly on the radar. Only thirty-five years old and running above 70% operational efficiency for my entire working life, I was in my prime in every way. Obviously I took special care with my own statistics during planning and pro-actively addressed any failings long before they manifested themselves. She must be wrong.

She was getting impatient. "What is wrong with you? This is an unbelievable honour."

I must admit I was doubtful about that. The need to move on when you were unable to do your job properly was a duty that all should observe, but an honour? Hardly.

"Would you like me to explain it slowly?" She was talking like a mentor to an apeman.

Sarcastic or condescending, I did not know, but best go along with it. "Yes please Ms Ferrante."

The Manager slid smoothly to my work table and perched on my high stool. She hitched her feet underneath herself with toes on the rest and leaned forward resting her forearms on her knees. The impression was close, supporting and conspiratorial – all of which were probably designed into that pose at Manager School. I felt warm and safe though.

"A crime has been committed. A very serious crime." She paused, maybe to see if I understood such complicated sentences. I nodded seriously.

"Our process allows for a trial if the accused is Manager or Service..."

What else is there? I thought.

"... and they claim to be innocent of the charge." Another pause and I nodded again.

"The accused is provided with a lawyer and an advocate. The advocate's job is to gather arguments for the defence lawyer and you have been selected as that advocate." She paused for reaction but all I could return was a blank stare.

Ms Ferrante spun on the stool and alt-logged into my screen behind her. She flicked through to Ship Policies, found the page she wanted and sent to my inbox. Logging herself out, she turned back to the blank geneticist.

"This has everything you need to know about your part in this affair. The specifics: I am not permitted to discuss with you. You must get those from your ... err, your ..., your client."

Her indecision was incongruous enough for me to crawl out of my stupor. "Err?"

"Yes" she replied. "Apemen are normally just dispatched forthwith as guilt or innocence is irrelevant. This is a special case for a number of Management reasons, so you will treat it as though it were a service human. From a legal sense only, of course."

I have to admit; the fact that I had just been saved from retirement, with maybe forty more years to live, was the foremost thought on my mind. But I would deal with the information she had given so far straight away. "Management reasons" were clearly code for "not telling you more".

"But Anthony."

"Yes?"

"You might want to check on the Sleepers before you start."

Sleepers? I didn't know what that meant, but given my small portfolio assumed she was referring to the embryo vault.

"Yes Ma'am. I'll do that straight away."

She put her right arm out horizontally, palm sideways, as though she was waiting for me to give her a flask of reagents. While I considered that elegant object, she reached over with her other hand, grabbed my right hand and offered it to hers in a mirror image and shook them both. "Thank you Anthony, I wish you luck."

"You can call me Anthony." I stuttered then started punching myself in the leg as her back receded through the door.

Apeman

❖

Given a direct order from Management, I was keen to delay not one second. Success in such a task carries a 300% weighting so could give me a near five percent hike to my weekly efficiency rating. I had no idea what the advocacy job would deliver, but that could wait for now.

The first check was with Maintenance.

I felt like a Leader walking through the corridors during work time. There was nobody there to watch my Glorious March all the way to Jonathan's cubicle so I just snarled at an apeman that was sweeping up. It cowered with suitable deference so I graced it with a regal wave and continued on my way.

I bipped Jonathan's door and immediately hear a muffled crash followed by a very human exclamation and another heavier crash. Jonathan appeared at the entrance while small sounds of the aftermath were still in the air.

"Anthony?" He pushed his head and shoulders past me into the corridor and scanned both ways, at the same time pulling me into the room. "What the hell?"

I wanted to grace him just like the cleaner, but was immediately distracted by his amazing room. "It's OK. I have orders." was all I said. The cubicle was smaller than mine but unbelievably spacious. It contained just a table, chair and screen then wide open space to all the walls. All except one wall were bare Cellform and that wall comprised rows of bright red boxes on racks. One of the boxes was clearly responsible for the earlier mayhem, lying open on the floor with its entrails spilled around itself. It was an antique tiered concertina toolbox and the spill an assortment of inscrutable metal and carbon shapes. I suppressed a surge of unaccountable avarice and pulled myself back to the task in hand. "I need a status on the vault."

"A status? You get that in your feed every four hours, why the hell do you need to come down here for that?"

I realised my error. Thank Newton I hadn't visited Behaviour or some other department that would mark me down for my arrogance; but Jonathan would have to report the visit so I needed to cover up. "I am acting as Advocate in a serious crime. This is a client confidentiality matter."

Jonathan's face changed like a Learner who had just been told he might become an embryologist if he worked hard. He nodded in a "I understand how serious this is and will do my best to help" way. "Bullshit!" is what he said.

"So?"

"So read your feed. Use my screen if you really need to be here."

As Jonathan attended to his messed up toys on the floor I checked the maintenance log on his session. He even had access to current status so I had a look at that too and everything was green.

"Look, I really need your help with this, mate. Everything looks good but Management have told me to check on the embryos as though they know something. Is there something wrong here that I can't see?"

I like to think the "mate" made the difference, but it was probably the mention of Management. Anyway, Jonathan rose and joined me. He shoved me aside and took over at the screen. Two minutes of flashing around pages and spinning down rows of figures, he ended back at the 'current status' pie-chart I had previously found.

"All tickly-boop." And he locked the screen. "Look, if they found something wrong with the systems they would have come to me, not an egg-man. Why don't you look at your stuff instead? Maybe everyone is a ging-er now or they've evolved into rocket engineers?"

I was determined not to react. "Thank you Jonathan, you have been most helpful." Yes, I could speak like Management.

Gerald St Clare

As I walked back, I scoured my brain for exactly what Ms Ferrante had said. "Sleepers", she called them. "Look at the Sleepers"? Verbal orders were unheard of and now I knew why. But Jonathan may be right, what would I be expected to look at that nobody else could? And how would she already know there is something I should look at?

The only process on the ship that gave Management more access than I had was Termination. I didn't need to read the Court Policies to know how Termination worked.

In the old days on Earth (and on pre-teen Arkships), everyone carried their ancestry personally. Women would be born with all the eggs they would ever produce already hidden away in their own ovaries. Men were only equipped with little factories for creating sperm, but still they carried those factories around with them for their whole fertile life. So when people died, their entire future ancestry would be terminated as well. Siblings, parents and existing children would go on, but new direct descendants would be no more.

This feature of humans was an important consideration in Capital Punishment. One of the purposes of the death penalty was to clean up the human genome, removing recessive elements from humanity. Anyone descended from a heinous criminal should also be terminated when the criminal was executed and this was first honestly reflected in legislation that prevented donor sperm and eggs from the condemned from being used. Although it was not considered moral to also kill the children of the condemned, social and financial penalties were applied to the families to ensure they had lower success rates in society; we let Social Evolution take care of our moral problems.

Planet-based justice also had the concept of incarceration. I'm not clear how it worked but apparently criminals were locked in boxes for a period of time depending on the severity of their crime. During that time they were not allowed to be productive. This is all very confusing to me as it seems there is a cost to maintaining all those boxes but no benefit.

I arrived at my door but didn't go in. I dared not go in yet. I took the unprecedented luxury of a stroll round the Ring while I explored my thoughts.

So the Arkships dispensed with the ridiculous idea of incarceration. A minor infraction like strolling around instead of working would give you a hit on your efficiency rating. More serious problems that affect the ship directly could give you a complete zero for the week. But none of these were crimes. The Policies had an 80 page definition of what constitutes a crime - and all were punishable by death.

And when an execution was carried out, Management would instigate the automated process to select all embryos related to the condemned and fry them.

It would take me another fifteen minutes to complete the whole Ring walk, so I turned 180 degrees and rushed back to my lab.

I was immensely relieved to be wrong.

It seemed so clear that the only possible answer to Ms Ferrante's enquiry was that someone had issued a Terminate order. Normally I would receive a Notification of Completion so that I could go and clean up all the dead embryos on that family tree, but there wasn't one in my Inbox. I also realised that a hacker may not have Management access so would trigger the Termination event at a lower level. Such a hack would not give me a notification and if it was clever enough, not even a system warning. I had no need to talk to the Systems Department to check on that, I could just check the embryos.

So I ran a diagnostic on all families and only Jones was showing orange on temperature. That was a glitch that had been hanging around for months, they were all fine. Or were they? I did a single-diag check on Jones and they all showed alive and green. Yes all was well in the vault.

Then a funny thought hit me. If they want to treat the apeman as a legal human, it would be subject to Termination, not just a dispatch. Apemen who went wrong were just thrown in the furnace, they were already recessive so no need to terminate the genome (i.e. all apemen). Which embryos would be affected?

I ran the test.

None.

I checked my query and ran the test again.

None.

What had I done wrong? I must have stared at the screen for ten minutes. I had no idea. I knew I was really good with queries: a mistake could be catastrophic so I always took extra care. So I checked again bringing the full force of my Query Logic courses to bear on it. I noticed that the request I had made was syntactically the same as "All living apeman". The best check is to throw in a "NOT" experiment, so I amended it to "NOT All living apeman", no that's stupid, "All (NOT living) apeman".

4581 results.

"Shit! They're all dead!"

I copied the ID of the first row and sent it to the vault monitor. One of the cameras spun to the location and there it was - a tiny red light in an array of healthy dark spots. I requested "Eject" and confirmed with my password. The little tube would arrive at the lab within a few minutes so I set to my designated Legal reading.

Security was represented by Gregory Phillips, a huge but charming gentleman who seemed genuinely concerned for my safety. He fussed around me making sure all the buckles were secure.

"Kevlar can only protect your major organs. There is nothing we can do to stop the perp' stabbing you in the eye if you won't wear the glasses."

"I'm sorry, Gregory, it's important for us to have eye-to-eye contact."

"Okay, but just keep enough distance so that you can push the button if it makes a move." He was referring to a squeeze-bulb that had been glued to my palm. He gave it a firm yank that hurt like a bad burn, but it didn't move. "Ouch!"

"Yeah, you'll say worse than ouch if it falls off."

"And you will come in if I hit the alarm?"

"Alarm? What alarm?"

I waved my hand in his face.

"That's not an alarm. Squeeze that and you zap its brain. It pumps a neurotoxin straight into its grey stuff: immediate paralysis then heart failure and asphyxiation in a couple of minutes."

I immediately cast a straight arm salute, determined it stay flat and open until I returned to Gregory.

"Yeah, very funny." He was unimpressed.

I put my hand behind my back in embarrassment.

"Right. Are you right?"

"Right." I said (what brilliant repartee).

Gregory grabbed the back of my armour like it was a handle and lifted me to a standing position. He then drove me like a vacuum cleaner to the cell door, hit the code and shoved me in as soon as the opening was nearly wide enough for me. I looked back over my shoulder and it was already closing as his hand withdrew. Cautiously I returned my attention to the room.

The cell was identical in size to my lab but even more impressively expansive than Jonathan's room. The wall behind me was all mirrored with only the Cellform door breaking into the reflection, all other walls were just Cellform. The far wall sported a fold-down cot and pedestal toilet and in the exact centre of the room was an alloy lab table with a low chair on either side.

And in the far chair facing me was the brutish form of the apeman. Clothed in its standard scarlet one-piece it leaned slightly forward with elbows on the table. Its paws were clasped together, probably due to the manacles with chains disappearing into a hole in the centre of the table. The head and face were almost naked of fur which had been hacked back to a dark shadow. It's eyes glared at me with a malevolent intelligence.

I had no idea if apemen had names or what sort of language they spoke. "Yessir." was all I'd ever got in any apeman exchange up to that day,

"Do you have a name I can use?" I asked.

me called thog

I can handle this. "Hello Thog. Do you know why we are here?"

"No, really Mr Farrah, please call me Martin." Its voice had transformed into an impersonation of Samuel the librarian. "And why start with such a complex question? Why are we here on this vessel? What is our ultimate purpose? I suspect you meant to ask what is my predicament."

The mimicry was astounding. From a human, that would have just sounded like showing off; but from this brute it must have been a feat of memory and vocal contortion.

"Yes, predicament." I replied doubtfully.

It nodded slowly. "I am accused of killing a few thousand embryos from the vault."

"And you are innocent?" I knew this was so because the hack was well beyond its abilities.

"No, I killed them."

"By mistake?"

"No, very deliberately. I killed them because..."

I interrupted immediately. "No, don't tell me that. I'd like to explain why I am here."

"Metaphysically?"

"No." I was definitely becoming unnerved by the apeman's use of language, he was not mimicking anyone.

"Thank Newton for that!" He grinned at me.

"The crime you are charged with carries the death

penalty, but you are permitted a trial if you claim to be innocent. Whether you actually did it or not does not matter to the court, it's all about which side provides the most compelling arguments."

"I am no innocent, but I am innocent of the charges. I have murdered nobody."

"OK. We'll see if you still think that after I explain. But we are agreed that you will claim to be innocent and I will work on arguments supporting that. So the details:"

I explained the way the trial would be run. Two identical GV34 AI units had been uploaded with Lawyer programming, each with full access to the central database of Case Law. One was designated Prosecution with instructions to argue against the accused, the other was designated Defence for the converse reason. Arguments would be prepared by the advocates: I was the defence advocate and someone else (we don't know who) would be the prosecution advocate. Only the lawyers were permitted to appear and speak in court (except for the final statement from the accused) and they would use arguments as appropriate based on case law and the direction of the trial. The trial would be heard and judgement made by one of the Managers and the penalty enacted only if both lawyers agreed that the judgement was consistent with the arguments presented. If my client was found guilty, his implant would immediately be activated and he would be dead in a few minutes. His unborn family would be immediately withdrawn from availability and terminated within one week.

I had not yet told him that he had messed up his mass-murder attempt, killing his own siblings instead of whoever the real target was. Surely not the Leaders?

"So now I have to talk with the lawyer bot and see what sort of defence we can mount. I'll come back to you soon for more information if that's OK?"

"Should I wait here?" He lightly rattled his chains in demonstration of the absurdity.

I stood and turned to the back wall, confused because Gregory had not told me how to call him after the meeting was over.

"Just walk to the door." Martin could read my mind as well as Ms Ferrante. I complied and the door swished aside just as I was about to bash my nose on it.

"And can you get proper shaving gear for me?" He called as it closed behind me.

The idea of a meeting with a robot was as ridiculous as it sounds. The AI was perfectly capable of reading a mail and responding to it, so this ceremony made little sense to me. Not expecting any response I asked the lawyer directly.

"Protocol dictates that you provide the arguments complete and intact in every sense. I am only permitted to interpret them in the context of Case Law. To this end, it is your responsibility to deliver them accurately as repeatable statements, including nuance and other attributes only delivered through speech. If, for instance, the argument is driven by anger or love you must shout or whisper angrily or lovingly. I am not equipped to do this."

I needed more guidance. "I have never done this before. What sort of arguments can I make?"

"The easiest way to start is to look at any available evidence."

"So I find proof that he is innocent." I didn't see how I could become a detective overnight.

"Evidence is not proof. It is only a suggestion of a fact. Once you find evidence, your job is to construct an argument that presents that evidence favourably to your client's case."

"So what evidence do we have so far?"

I'm sure the bot was being critical of me. "You have

not provided any, but fortuitously all evidence must be shared so we already have the hack details including target population, source terminal and login ID."

"Which screen?"

"GenLab. Your terminal"

"And you know who was logged on? And what they did?"

"Yes, a standard Termination request was made by Female C1197/44 just before noon, four days ago on family name 'apeman'"

Was Martin covering up for Rozinia Ferrante? That one sentence gave me so many questions I was not ready to share yet, but one thing I knew: "That wouldn't work. 'apeman' is not a family name."

"That is all the evidence we have. It is your job to develop it into legal arguments."

Walking the corridors while others worked had become a habit for me. I felt a sense of power in this act of nonconformity that was otherwise impossible to all but Managers. The license I had assumed raised me to my own personal caste, certainly not usurping Management but above those lowly Service personnel who mindlessly ploughed their tiny, closed portfolios.

The power you have over someone with a door blip was invigorating. With just a press of a button, you could demand their immediate attention and they were compelled to physically attend to your needs by walking to the door and granting "open". I can only imagine the parasitised Olympian energy of the old-earthers equipped with portable devices that could issue these commands remotely.

The door was answered with the usual blend of confusion, anger and concern. Even I used to be like that in the old days. "Anthony?"

"Hello Daniel. I am under orders from Management to advocate on a serious crime and I need your help." My script was getting much more slick and commanding.

"Of course, Anthony. Come in. How can I help?"

Oh the power...

"Have you heard about the hack from four days ago?"

"Hack? No, there has been no hack." He seemed quite sure of that. I tried a look that didn't quite work. "That I know about..." Better.

Apeman

I walked to his stool and settled myself in it. I had seen this pose delivered by an expert. "The Termination request on family 'apeman'"

"Yes, I saw that and it went through with no problem."

That was not what I expected. Daniel was supposed to scurry off and dig around in bytes to find out how it had happened. "But 'apeman' is not a family, it's a species."

"Well you are the biologist so I'll take your word on that but from a data point of view we don't have a special field for them, they are just tagged with that in the d_family column. As they don't have a family per se, we just reuse the field." He stopped and inspected a spot between my eyes then realised I needed more. "To all intents and purposes the only thing that differentiates apemen is that they have family name 'apeman'. Databases are funny like that."

"So it would take special Systems knowledge to know how to do this."

"Yes, or just a naive attacker who thinks 'apeman' is a family."

Great! I find an alternative suspect and he casts doubt in five seconds.

I didn't bother with an appointment for my second visit to Martin. Gregory jumped to attention on my arrival and bustled over with my costume. "It's loose in its cell, so you'll have to wait while I chain it up."

"HE!" I was taking no truck with that. "He is free in his cell and we do not need chains, armour or arbitrary execution devices. I would like to talk with my client."

The big man was blown backwards with the force of my determination. Well, actually he just slowed down a bit before trying to wrap me in kevlar. I pushed him away and he allowed me to succeed. "Is that a formal request?"

I looked up to address the room camera. "Confirmed". And walked to the cell door which stayed shut. I knocked with two sharp raps just as Gregory tapped in the code.

"Come in." Martin seemed genuinely touched by the gesture. He was sitting on the cot but rose and approached me with his hand extended just like Ms Ferrante had done. I examined it for long enough that he just put it in his pocket instead of grabbing me.

I got straight to the point. "Do you know Rozinia Ferrante?"

"No. But my guess is tall, hazel eyes, long brown, slightly coppery hair twenty-fiveish, nose a little crooked. And did I mention the eyes? Beautiful, deep, truly the windows to the soul."

"You don't know her?"

"No"

I was exasperated. "Why do you play with me like this?"

"I'm not. Four syllables means Manager. Woman's name. There are two female Managers, one old, one young. My guess is that you would be interested in the beautiful young one. The one with login ID rozzie44?"

"You don't know her but you know her login ID?"

He tugged a flapping corner of his bright red suit. "I have an invisibility cloak that lets me go places other can't"

I felt his need to show off was destroying my attempts to help him. "You are only making this worse. Everything you say can only be used to condemn you."

"But I did it. I know you are trying to frame that Manager to get me off, but who am I to allow someone else to fall in my place? No. I take responsibility for what I did and will pay any price that is placed on the act."

"So how do I do my job? You won't let me fight for an innocent verdict and there is no leeway on sentence so

I can't plead for half an execution based in diminished responsibility or something. I want to help you!"

"I tried to tell you why I did it and you brushed me off. Are you ready to hear it now?"

He was impossible! "No! I'm not going to take some terrorist manifesto to the court. Shut up and let me work on something positive." I turned round and walked smack into the door.

"He has to release it first, walk more slowly." Martin gently helped me to my feet, gave a thumbs up to the mirror and backed all the way to his cot. As soon as he sat down, the door opened.

My only excuse was that Martin had enraged me and I was not thinking clearly but the door was already open and I could not turn back. I had found myself up on the Nose-ward Ring accommodation section with my thumb on the door button of a Manager's private suite.

She stood in front of me, uncertain like a child and dressed in a blue service one-piece just like mine. I noticed that her hair was, indeed, coppery but now frizzy at the edges like an electrified halo. She had a tired look on her face. No, tired was not right. But her energy looked dissipated. Martin was right, she was beautiful.

"You can take your finger off it. It's binary." She pointed at my hand pressed against the door jamb. "And come in." She disappeared from the anteroom, walking deeper into the suite.

I followed her into a cosy room with four stuffed chairs and a little table with a reading light. She had settled into the chair nearest the light where she must have been reading from her detached screen. With a wave I was invited to sample one of the other chairs. I tried it and liked it a lot.

I had to brazen this out so didn't hesitate. "Why wasn't the apeman just dispatched like the Policies dictate?"

"Has he told you why he did it?"

Did she just say 'He'? "My client will plead innocent of the charge on all counts. He has clearly stated to me that he has murdered nobody."

She replied in a soothing tone. "It's all right Anthony, no recording takes place in Manager suites. You can speak honestly."

"No, I am not interested in his manifesto as it has no bearing on the case."

"If that is true, then your question also has no bearing. You have no need to know why the trial is taking place."

She wasn't going to twist it so easily. "As advocate, I am the only one who can decide what is relevant to my client's case"

She laughed. "Well played advocate!" I felt a thrill of satisfaction. "But you are wrong, the two are linked."

"So this is revenge for his attempt to implicate you?" A huge assumption but worth a punt.

"Quite the opposite, Anthony. Once I worked out why he did it, I wished I could have had the courage to run the command myself. Subsequently, the least I could do was let him have a voice."

This was all wrong. I didn't know what to ask so just prompted her. "Go on..."

"Dispatching is silent, anonymous. The whole thing would just go away quietly. Your client – what's his name?"

"Martin" She is asking for his name? This is surreal!

"Martin and his family have been disenfranchised for generations. He and they have now paid the ultimate price and I cannot let that come to nothing. Go and listen to him. You are his voice now."

I assumed I was being dismissed so gave her a subtle bow and rose to leave.

"Just one more thing Anthony."

"Yes?"

"If you try to use anything we discussed here, I will deny it. You have to do this on your own."

"Yes, Ma'am. I understand" I left with my head spinning.

I still had nothing for the lawyer so went straight back to Martin. Gregory just flicked his head toward an upper corner of his office as I entered so I faced the camera up there with "I take full responsibility for my actions despite the best efforts of Security to protect my safety."

"Zero zero zero one" was Gregory's offhand response, which I used on the keypad to let myself in.

"What, no knock?" Martin asked amiably.

"I'm sorry, I wasn't thinking."

"Relax, I'm not bothered as long as you don't mind catching me banging one out."

Apeman humour was a little base for my taste. "I'm ready to hear why you did it."

He clapped his hands together. "There is hope for you yet, Mr Farrah."

"Well, you have friends in high places."

"How sweet."

"So?"

"Slavery is an abomination to mankind"

"and hands that shed innocent blood?" I really didn't expect him to recognise the quote.

"Yes, well. I'm not too concerned about what that megalomaniac finds abominable. He's probably the biggest ever historic cause of slavery."

I was impressed. "You mentioned Newton, are you a member of Fema?" No response. "Or any other religious group?"

He laughed a hearty and generous guffaw. "Apemen don't form groups, we have to think independently. You may have noticed I read more than most?"

I agreed. He seemed to be more well-read than any human I knew. Correction: any other human I knew.

"Well, I read just enough to have informed opinions."

"So you think you are a slave and took vengeance on your slavers? Well I have some news for you, apeman!" I flared up in anger for the tiny helpless sparks he had snuffed out. "You killed the wrong ones You killed all the apemen instead of the Leaders."

I didn't get the reaction of horror or submission I expected. Martin seemed unsurprised."

"What do you have in your precious vault Anthony?"

I railed at the use of my first name but ignored the deliberate barb. "Embryos"

"No, not embryos. You are the geneticist: what are they?"

"Human embryos." What was he getting at?

"Step by step. But you're not being honest with yourself. You have about twenty million Carnegie Stage 1, pre-blastomer zygotes (sorry if I'm mashing your terminology on that one)."

I shook my head, I understood what he meant: first week embryos.

Martin continued. "It would have been so much easier to just carry eggs and sperm and fertilise them in flight as needed but you then have no basis for differentiating bloodlines. Every single one of those cells in the honeycomb is a fertilised egg. The mother and father are already known, the genetic code merged, but cell division has not yet started. Our founders have given us a predetermined social heritage but still the ability to tinker.

And you do tinker, don't you?"

What was he accusing me of? "Yes, of course. We check for congenital diseases straight after call-off and make genetic corrections before the cell is brought up to temperature and allowed to divide."

"And?"

"And nothing. We protect the child from harm."

"And my family?"

Ah, the family thing again... "What about them?"

"Tinkering?"

"Yes, we have to add genetic markers to make you physically recognisable as apemen."

"Stronger muscles?"

"No"

"Brow ridges and a shambling gait?"

"Of course not. Just facial hair. Otherwise you are identical to us."

He just sat there and looked at me. A deep and demanding look. I realised I was giving him a win with the long pause and just started to speak when he continued. "I'm disappointed in you Anthony. Maybe you need some time to think about what you just said."

No I knew. I had always known. But I was one of the privileged, not one of them. We had to do what was necessary to differentiate the good and the bad. They were bad and had always been bad but now we didn't have to worry about them any more. He had done us a service and removed our evil side. I had my arguments for the trial!

"So you always meant to murder your entire species?"

"I told you Anthony. I murdered nobody. We just withdrew our labour."

I thought I had done so well with the brilliant main argument. Realising that Ms Ferrante was on our side I soon worked out that the key was her decision to try Martin as Service. The lawyer just ridiculed my brilliance.

"The law just doesn't work like that Mr Farrah. If you

try to say the law is an ass it will kick you back in the appropriate bodily area."

I felt that Daniel in Systems needed to go back to the drawing board for the humour subroutines. "I'm not saying any such thing, it's logically solid."

"Well, if that is your main argument, I suggest you recite it now for me to record. I recommend an Academic tone with an undercurrent of pragmatism. Please start when you are ready."

I cleared an imaginary obstruction in my throat and did my best Mentor impersonation.

"My client admits a crime was committed and agrees that, as the only available suspect, he should be executed forthwith as the law dictates. The law further dictates that all his line must be Terminated within a week of this judgement. The outcome of these two events is that there are no offspring for him to have murdered, thus necessitating a pardon in one week's time. I request that the charges be dismissed forthwith to save one further unnecessary death."

"Thank you Mr Farrah. I'll send a transcript for you to practice that one. Maybe you would like to lose the supercilious tone and come back for another try?"

I only hoped my counterpart was having as hard a time

with the tin-top as I was.

"But that 'righteous purging of the evil bloodline' argument is probably worth developing, even though it doesn't play well with this one."

A week later it was done. Two weeks later I was sitting in my lab considering it.

The defence lawyer had played up a deep religious conviction in the apeman, culminating in its delusion that some form of slavery was in use on the ship and that it was one such slave. Although it did not admit to being the cause of the species extinction, the accused sympathised with the need to end the practice and offered its own life to make amends. He also tested my logic bomb as a hypothetical and was warned by the judge that he would be held in contempt if he wished to offer it as an argument.

The prosecution simply offered the apeman's work schedule as evidence, demonstrating how easily it could have both overseen a Manager login and freely entered my lab. They also pointed out that even though the apeman was being tried as a Service person, that was a political decision and did not affect its nature. Any claim that the apeman was Service caste, indeed that it was even human, should be rejected.

They had sent me the transcript of the statement from the accused and that was currently displayed on my lab screen:

> *I base my case on the ancient law that is an intrinsic part of the Constitution we use when settling new worlds:*
>
> *"No one shall be held in slavery or servitude; slavery and the slave trade shall be prohibited in all their forms." [Universal (sic) Declaration of Human Rights, Article 4]*
>
> *This inalienable right is enshrined in all the freedoms included in our Constitution, from Innate Freedom, discrimination, right to life, (I could name so many more) right up to the right to equal treatment under the law. I suggest to the Court that whatever Society considers me (and my family) to be, our position on this Arkship is certainly a form of slavery. By being excluded from nearly all of the the constitutional provisions, there can be no other interpretation.*
>
> *And the prohibition is not just on a particular version of slavery, but specifically includes "all its forms". In ancient times, clever arguments would be used to disenfranchise selected groups – with billions locked into enforced servitude for the benefit of a few. That wording of our Consitution was specifically designed to deal with such double-talk.* **Any** *form of slavery is prohibited.*

Apeman

> *But through my actions (which I do not deny), I have removed the ability for our Society to continue with this practice. If I am not a slave (as I am sure the prosecution will argue), then I have the right to withdraw my labour. However, if I am a slave then I have a duty to withdraw my labour in order to protect the Constitution. The terrible act of terminating my entire line ensures that this cannot continue. If my life is the price I have to pay, then it is a small price for the good of our whole society.*

Manager C1197/44 was given a one month zero against her efficiency rating for allowing her password to be compromised.

Martin Apeman was executed four hours after the hearing ended.

The good news was that the Jones glitch was sorted out. Genealogy had found that the female parent of the Jones line may have been descended from a mutant from one of the nuclear disasters of the twenty-first century. Daniel's database update was a two minute job before I could start the first order for mutants. And the orange temperature light? I just pulled the offending mutant from the honeycomb and threw it in the waste.

Now I just had to design a mutant marker that was as obvious as facial hair.

Gerald St Clare

I want to sail away to a distant shore and make like an ape man.

[The Kinks]